Welcome to ALADDIN QUIX!

If you are looking for fast, fun-to-read stories with colorful characters, lots of kid-friendly humor, easy-to-follow action, entertaining story lines, and lively illustrations, then **ALADDIN QUIX** is for you!

But wait, there's more!

If you're also looking for stories with tables of contents; word lists; about-the-book questions; 64, 80, or 96 pages; short chapters; short paragraphs; and large fonts, then **ALADDIN QUIX** is *definitely* for you!

ALADDIN QUIX: The next step between ready to reads and longer, more challenging chapter books, for readers five to eight years old.

Read more ALADDIN QUIX books!

A Miss Mallard Mystery
By Robert Quackenbush

A Miss Mallard Mystery

DOGSLED TO DREAD

ROBERT QUACKENBUSH

ALADDIN QUIX

New York London Toronto Sydney New Delhi

ALADDIN QUIX

Simon & Schuster Children's Publishing Division

1230 Avenue of the Americas, New York, New York 10020

This Aladdin QUIX paperback edition September 2019

Copyright © 1987 by Robert Quackenbush

Also available in an Aladdin QUIX hardcover edition.

All rights reserved, including the right of reproduction in whole or in part in any form.

ALADDIN and the related marks and colophon are registered trademarks of Simon & Schuster, Inc.

For information about special discounts for bulk purchases, please contact Simon & Schuster Special Sales at 1-866-506-1949 or business@simonandschuster.com.

The Simon & Schuster Speakers Bureau can bring authors to your live event. For more information or to book an event contact the Simon & Schuster Speakers Bureau at 1-866-248-3049 or visit our website at www.simonspeakers.com.

Designed by Tiara Iandiorio

The illustrations for this book were rendered in pen and ink and wash.

The text of this book was set in Archer Medium.

Manufactured in the United States of America 0819 OFF

2 4 6 8 10 9 7 5 3 1

Library of Congress Control Number 2019931557

ISBN 978-1-5344-1421-1 (hc)

ISBN 978-1-5344-1420-4 (pbk)

ISBN 978-1-5344-1422-8 (eBook)

First for Piet and Margie,
and especially for the schoolchildren I visited in
Anchorage, Alaska.
And now for Emma and Aiden.

Cast of Characters

Miss Mallard: World-famous ducktective

Vera and Arnold Drake: Heads of the local business group in Duckton

Nina: Husky who is lead dog in the Duckton dogsled race

Sheriff Ruddy-Duck: Duckton's law officer

Totem-Masked Glacier Avenger: The mischief-maker responsible for the recent trouble in Duckton

Ben Scoter: Nina's trainer

George Scaup: A sled driver in the Duckton race

Jed Merganzer: Owner of the Welcome gift shop

What's in Miss Mallard's Bag?

Miss Mallard has many detective tools she brings with her on her adventures around the world.

In her knitting bag she usually has:

- Newspaper clippings
- Knitting needles and yarn
- A magnifying glass
- A flashlight
- A mirror
- A travel guide
- Chocolates for her nephew

Contents

1

Alaskan Adventure

Miss Mallard, the world-famous ducktective, looked up at the enormous stuffed polar bear in the **lounge** of the hotel where she was staying.

She shivered and said to **Vera**

and Arnold Drake, "I can't get over the huge size of things here in Alaska. It is all so **rustic** and beautiful—it's like going back to the old **frontier** days. Thank you so much for inviting me here."

"We're so glad you could come," said Vera, who was knitting a long woolen scarf.

"As the heads of the local business group here in Duckton," she continued, "Arnold and I have been working a long time to get you here. We were grateful you

could change your plans at the last minute."

"We couldn't think of a better duck to open the dogsled races tomorrow," said Arnold. "Duckton's **annual** races draw a bigger crowd than the races held in Anchorage. There will be a lot of news coverage."

"How exciting!" said Miss Mallard. "I **launched** a ship once but never a dogsled race."

They looked out the large picture window at the huskies and

their trainers gathering outside. This was their last chance to practice for the races the following day.

"See the husky with her puppies?" Vera pointed outside. "That's **Nina**. She has won every race for the past three years. She is sure to win again this year. She has been **friskier** than ever since her puppies were born."

"She's a real champion!" added Arnold.

2

Dognapped!

Miss Mallard watched out the lounge window as Nina was being buckled in. She was the lead dog for her sled.

Her puppies were nearby. They were playing in the snow.

Suddenly, a costumed figure on skis came tearing down the mountain. It swooped to grab a puppy and then vanished into the woods.

"Great **tundra**!" cried Arnold. "One of Nina's puppies has been dognapped! Quick, Vera, call **Sheriff Ruddy-Duck**!"

In her rush to get a phone, Vera dropped her knitting. Miss Mallard helped her pick it up and shove it into her bag.

Then Miss Mallard grabbed

her own knitting bag, where she kept her detective tools. She ran outside with Arnold.

Outside, there was confusion everywhere. Nina and the other huskies were howling and bark-ing. Their trainers were racing around quacking and trying to calm them.

"The **Totem-Masked Glacier Avenger** has struck again!" cried one of the trainers.

3

Revenge!

Miss Mallard asked Arnold, "Who is the Totem Avenger?"

Arnold replied, "Months ago he sent a note to our sheriff. He said he would make everyone pay for some wrong that had been done.

"Ever since, he has been scaring our town. He wears the costume of a **totem pole**," Arnold explained.

"One time he ruined a hockey match by sprinkling salt on the ice—the players kept tripping and falling," he continued.

"I'm afraid, Miss Mallard, he has done much more—all of it bad—but this is the worst. And we have no idea when he will strike again," Arnold said.

"Oh no!" quacked Miss Mallard.

Just then Sheriff Ruddy-Duck arrived in his snowmobile. News of the dognapping had spread all over town, and a crowd gathered around him. He questioned the witnesses and made out a report.

"What are you going to do about this, Sheriff?" asked **Ben Scoter,** Nina's trainer.

"I'll send out an all-points bulletin right away on Nina's puppy," answered Sheriff Ruddy-Duck. "I will do everything I can to arrest the Totem Avenger."

With that, he put away his notebook and hurried off.

After the sheriff left, Ben Scoter turned to the crowd and said, "Did you hear that? The sheriff has been talking about a speedy arrest for months. But nothing has been done to stop the Totem Avenger. I say it is time we got a new sheriff in Duckton."

Everyone gasped!

"The one for the job," Ben Scoter continued, "is Arnold Drake. At least he and Vera brought Miss

Mallard here to work on the case."

"Good idea!" said some Arnold supporters.

Miss Mallard was surprised.

"Is that true?" she asked Vera and Arnold. "Is that the *real* reason you invited me to Alaska?"

They both blushed and nodded their heads.

"But we still want you to start the race tomorrow," said Arnold.

"We believed you might think that our troubles in Duckton were not important enough," said Vera.

"We thought if we invited you as our guest to the races, you would be more likely to come."

"*Every* case is important to me," said Miss Mallard.

"Then you'll help us?" said Vera and Arnold together.

"Yes," said Miss Mallard. "I'll begin my investigations at once."

"Hooray! Hooray for Miss Mallard!" shouted the crowd.

4

A New Sheriff?

"Let's go to the hotel," said one of Arnold's supporters, "and make plans for Arnold to take over as sheriff."

Vera and Arnold led the way. The crowd followed them back

to the hotel, loudly chanting,

"ARNOLD DRAKE FOR SHERIFF! ARNOLD DRAKE FOR SHERIFF!"

Miss Mallard stayed behind with the huskies and their trainers. Ben Scoter was at her side.

She asked Ben, "Why do you think the Totem Avenger took one of Nina's puppies?"

"For only one reason," said Ben. "You can see how upset Nina is. She will be in no shape to run in the race tomorrow unless her puppy is found.

"If the puppy isn't found—and I have my **doubts** that it will be— then the other favored team is bound to win," he explained.

"Which team is that?" asked Miss Mallard.

"**George Scaup**'s team," said Ben.

"Are you saying that Scaup is to blame for what happened here today?" Miss Mallard asked him.

Ben answered, "Yes, I am."

George Scaup, who had been hiding behind a totem pole, ran toward them.

"I heard that, Ben!" he quacked. "I could take you to court for lying about me. I was here the whole time and you know it!"

"You could have easily hired someone!" Ben exclaimed.

"That does it!" said George. He started to take a swing at Ben.

Miss Mallard stood between the two, warning them, "Nina's puppy will *never* be found this way."

Ben tried to calm poor Nina, who was howling **mournfully** over the loss of her puppy. Grumbling,

George went back to his huskies.

Miss Mallard went to the spot where Nina's puppy had been grabbed. There were no clues. Even the Totem Avenger's ski tracks had been quickly covered by the falling snow.

But wait!

One of the other puppies was tugging on something that lay half-buried in the snow. He finally freed it and brought it to Miss Mallard.

It was a knitted glove! It was

exactly like the kind the Totem Avenger had been wearing. No doubt he had dropped it, and in all the confusion, no one had noticed it.

Miss Mallard examined the glove. It was **handmade**. "Maybe it came from the gift shop at the hotel," she thought. She went to investigate.

Inside the gift shop, she could hear loud talking from the lounge next door. It sounded as if Arnold would soon be the new sheriff.

Miss Mallard showed the glove to a salesperson. She asked if it had come from the shop.

"No" was the answer. "We don't carry handmade goods. You can try **Jed Merganzer**'s gift shop—it's called Welcome—or try the Portage Glacier Gift Shop. They are both within walking distance down the mountain. But you will have to wear snowshoes to get there."

"Thank you," said Miss Mallard as she left the shop.

5

Lost Glove

Outside, Miss Mallard put on a pair of the hotel's snowshoes and trudged down the mountain. At last she came to a crooked little house. The large sign over the door said **WELCOME.**

"This must be Jed Merganzer's shop," said Miss Mallard. She took off her snowshoes and walked in.

Everywhere she looked, the walls were covered with scraps of paper. Then she saw someone sitting behind a counter that displayed local handmade items.

"Are you Jed Merganzer?" asked Miss Mallard.

"Yep," said Jed. "What can I do for you?"

Miss Mallard held up the mysterious glove.

"I thought you might recognize this," she said. "Did it come from your store?"

"Never saw it before," said Jed.

Miss Mallard turned to leave when Jed added, "Pin your card on the wall. Everyone else does."

Old postcards, business cards, photos, and letters were pinned up all over.

Miss Mallard took out a business card. "I'll put it under this photo," she said. "I know the couple in this picture—Vera and Arnold

Drake. I guess nearly everybody has been in your store."

"That's right," said Jed sourly. "But most of them don't buy anything. I wish I had a dollar for every card folks have pinned up here. I would be a rich duck."

Miss Mallard thought he sounded angry and sad. She finished putting up her card, said good-bye, and hurriedly left.

Back in the cold, Miss Mallard put on her snowshoes and started off again.

After only a few steps, she thought she heard the dull sound of something moving. The sound came from a shed behind Jed's store.

She listened again. This time she heard a loud

CRUNCH!
CRUNCH!
CRUNCH!

She looked behind her and gasped.

6

Moose on the Loose

It was a huge moose!

"Nice moose," Miss Mallard whispered fearfully. Then she turned to run.

She *clumped, clumped* in her snowshoes as fast as she could.

At last, she came to the Portage Glacier Gift Shop. She ran inside and slammed the door.

"No snowshoes inside," said the clerk in the shop.

"Sorry," said Miss Mallard. "I was being chased by a moose. I'll leave as soon as he is gone. In the meantime, do you sell this kind of glove here?"

Once more she held up the mysterious glove.

"Absolutely not!" said the clerk.

Miss Mallard looked out the window. The moose was gone.

"Then I'll be on my way," she said.

As she went out the door, she heard the clerk sigh with relief.

Discouraged, Miss Mallard started back to the hotel. She stuffed the mysterious glove deep into her knitting bag.

From the bottom of the bag, some strands of yarn stuck to the mitten she was wearing. She looked at the strands in surprise.

"This is not my yarn," she said. "Where in the world did this come from?"

Then she remembered. She held the yarn next to the glove she had found. They matched exactly!

Suddenly everything was clear to Miss Mallard. She ran back to the gift shop and went inside. **"This is an emergency!"** she said. "I am Margery Mallard. I must use your phone!"

The clerk was thrilled to learn that the famous ducktective was in her shop. She offered to drive Miss Mallard to the hotel in a snowmobile after she called.

They arrived in a whirl of snow. Miss Mallard parked her snow-shoes and ran into the lounge.

The last **ballots** were just being counted to elect Arnold as the new sheriff of Duckton.

7

Puppy Love

"Hold everything!" said Miss Mallard to the voters. "This election must stop. The Totem Avenger has been unmasked."

"What do you mean, 'the Totem Avenger has been unmasked'?"

asked Vera and Arnold, puzzled.

"You will find out in just one minute," replied Miss Mallard.

All at once, a **squad** of snowmobiles pulled up. Out popped Sheriff Ruddy-Duck and his deputies. They had with them Jed Merganzer and Nina's puppy!

"Yahoo!" everyone yelled.

The crowd was wild with excitement and curiosity. They wanted to know what had happened.

"Without Miss Mallard," said Sheriff Ruddy-Duck, "this case

might not have been solved. She called and told me where to find the puppy. And she says Jed Merganzer is the Totem Avenger. How do you know that, Miss Mallard?"

"A bit of yarn did the trick," said Miss Mallard.

As soon as she said that, Vera and Arnold started to leave. **"Stop them, Sheriff,"** said Miss Mallard. "They are involved in this too."

When the crowd quieted down,

Miss Mallard said, "Here is the glove the Totem Avenger wore. It was knitted by Vera! I learned that when I found some **strands** of her yarn.

"Then," Miss Mallard added, "I remembered something about a photo I had seen in Jed's store. In the photo, Jed is wearing the glove."

Miss Mallard paused for breath. She went on, "Jed took Nina's puppy and hid it in his shed. But Vera and Arnold planned the

scheme. They even hired Jed to be the Totem Avenger!

"They also invited me here to make themselves look innocent. They wanted Arnold to be elected sheriff," she explained, "so they could take over the town. All Jed wanted was money."

"Deputies, take the crooks away," said Sheriff Ruddy-Duck.

Sheriff Ruddy-Duck and Miss Mallard returned the puppy to Nina.

It was a joyful reunion.

Ben Scoter and George Scaup were there. Ben said he was sorry for thinking George had anything to do with the crime and for wanting a new sheriff.

The two of them shook wings and made up. Then Nina gave Miss Mallard a big, wet, sloppy kiss.

SLURP!

"How can we ever thank you, Miss Mallard?" asked Sheriff Ruddy-Duck.

"Nina just did," said Miss Mallard.

Word List

annual (ANN·yoo·ul): Happening once a year

ballots (BAL·lets): Pieces of paper used to vote in an election

discouraged (dis·KUR·igd): Not feeling hopeful

doubts (DOWTS): Fears or uncertainties

friskier (FRIS·kee·er): More playful, energetic, and lively

frontier (frun·TEER): A faraway area where few people live

handmade (HAND·mayd):
Something made with hands or
hand tools, not by machine

launched (LONCHD): Began or
started

lounge (LOWNJ): A room or
area where people can wait or
relax

mournfully (MORN·ful·lee): Sadly

rustic (RUS·tick): Rural

scheme (SKEEM): A sneaky
plan or plot

squad (SKWAD): A small group
or team of people

strands (STRANDZ): Thin pieces of hair, yarn, or rope

totem pole (TOE·tem POLE): A tall, usually wooden pole carved and painted with symbols, figures, or masks that are related to one's family

tundra (TUN·druh): A large area of flat land where there are no trees and the ground is always frozen, usually in northern parts of the world

Questions

1. Which dog won the dogsled race for the past three years?

2. Why did Vera and Arnold Drake really invite Miss Mallard to Duckton?

3. Do you think George Scaup had anything to do with the dognapping?

4. Whose handmade glove did the puppy find in the snow?

5. Who was making the *CRUNCH! CRUNCH! CRUNCH!* sounds in the snow?

6. What clue in Miss Mallard's knitting bag helped her solve the case?

Acknowledgments

My thanks and appreciation go to Jon Anderson, president and publisher of Simon & Schuster Children's Books, and his talented team: Karen Nagel, executive editor; Karin Paprocki, art director; Tiara Iandiorio, designer; Elizabeth Mims, managing editor; Sara Berko, production manager; Tricia Lin, assistant editor; and Richard Ackoon, executive coordinator;

for launching out into the world again these incredible new editions of my Miss Mallard Mystery books for today's young readers everywhere.

CHUCKLE YOUR WAY THROUGH THESE EASY-TO-READ ILLUSTRATED CHAPTER BOOKS!

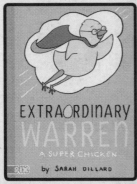

LOOKING FOR A FAST, FUN READ?
BE SURE TO MAKE IT ALADDIN QUIX!

EBOOK EDITIONS ALSO AVAILABLE

ALADDIN QUIX | SIMONANDSCHUSTER.COM/KIDS